MW01534457

The

Gift

of

Holiday Valley

JoAnn R. Forrester

ISBN: 978-1-937958-83-1
Library of Congress Control Number:
2014944378

Red Engine Press
Bridgeville, PA
Printed in the United States

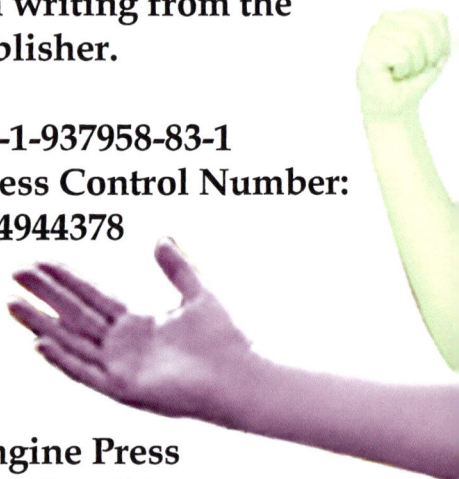

Once upon a time in a hidden valley called Holiday, there lived a little red-haired girl named Merry, who played every day with her best friend forever, Christmas.

Merry and Christmas spent many happy hours playing together in the land of Holiday. Soon people didn't say one name without the other. "Merry and Christmas," one of the parents would call, "it's time for dinner," or "it's time to do your homework," or "it's time to do your chores," (their least favorite call).

The two best friends shared the same birthday, December 25, and always celebrated together.

Their parents were friends and shared many happy times. This is how it was (and still is) in Holiday Valley. Friendships are special. Helping and sharing with others is important.

Merry was the more playful and adventuresome of the two. Christmas was quieter and more serious. Even though they were different, they loved to play and explore Holiday Valley.

One day Merry suggested "Let's climb to the top of the mountain and take a peek at the OUTSIDE. It will be fun."

"That's not a good idea," Christmas replied.

Only a few of the Olders had ever climbed to the top of the mountain and even fewer had been curious enough ... some called "foolhardy" enough ... to venture to the OUTSIDE.

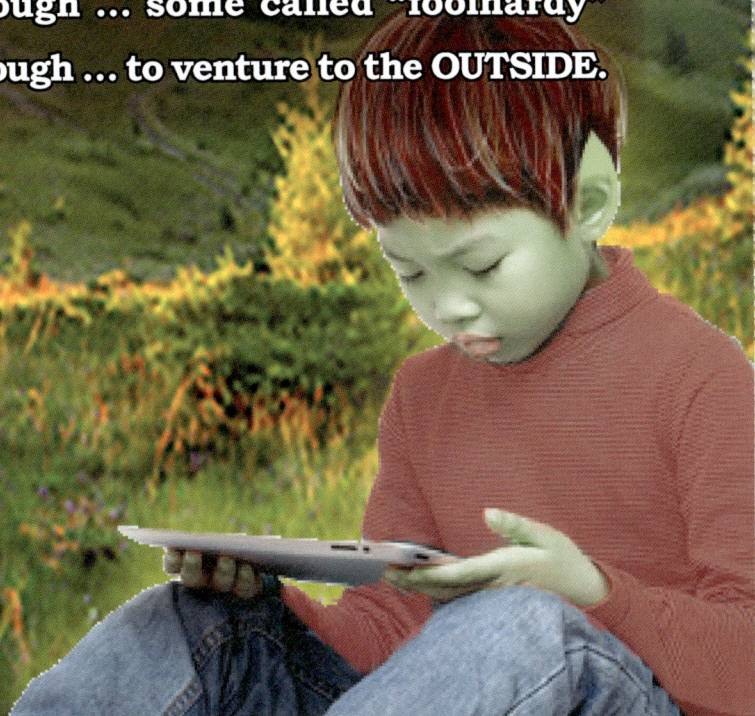

"Why not?" Merry wanted adventure.

"Because of what happened to my Great Uncle Jolly. He was the last Older to go to the OUTSIDE." The family loved to tell the story about Great Uncle Jolly and his journey. "When he was young and adventurous, Uncle Jolly decided to explore the OUTSIDE. He left the first day of spring and was gone a long, long time."

In fact, he was gone so long that most of the family had given up hope of seeing him again. Even though they sent messages and asked the visiting snow nomads (which is another story) who passed through every spring to find him — NO ONE could.

"Did he ever come back?"

"Finally ... but he looked sad and tired. He asked for a special meeting with the mayor and the Town Council. After many meetings and whispered discussions around town the mayor and the Holiday Council issued a SPECIAL OFFICIAL REPORT. They read it in the town square to all who came ... parents, grandparents, aunts, uncles, cousins, and all the animals of Holiday Valley.

"The Official Report said that the people of Holiday Valley were much safer and kinder than people on the OUTSIDE. It recommended that no one make trips to the OUTSIDE until conditions out there changed."

"That's why no one wants to go to the OUTSIDE, right?"

"Yes, people are happy here. We have many things to do and learn with friendly people." Christmas tried to persuade Merry to change her mind.

However, after much pleading and coaxing on Merry's part, Christmas agreed to go — as long as she promised not to cross over the dividing line between Holiday Valley and the OUTSIDE!

"I promise. I triple-dipple promise," Merry solemnly gave the never-ever-broken oath. That satisfied Christmas. They grabbed lots of snacks and some climbing supplies and off they went.

After searching a bit they found the path, which led to the top of the mountain. It took quite a while to climb the mountain, as large weeds, tall grass, and tree limbs covered the trail. It had been a long time since anyone tried to keep it neat and clean.

When they were close to the top, everything began to look downright spooky. Both children felt anxious and afraid. The sky seemed strange with its many different colors. The light faded. Cold dampness settled in and an odd smell filled the air. Something weird was happening!

They looked at each other and said, "Let's go home!"

They turned and headed down the path. All of a sudden a large ... no, a GIANT ... no, even bigger than GIANT ... a HUMONGOUS cloud descended on them. A thick red and green swirling mist expanded and rushed down the mountain. Merry and Christmas watched helplessly as it covered everyone and everything in its path. It was so dense that they could only see two feet ... no, one foot ahead.

Merry and Christmas were frightened. Did they cause this? Did the cloud come because they dared to walk up the path that led to the OUTSIDE? What was it doing to Holiday Valley? What was it doing to their parents, friends, and the animals? They started to climb down the mountain, but this time they had to tie ropes to one another so they wouldn't get lost in the swirling mist. It took them a long time to get home. They found everyone, even the animals, frightened and MAD!

This cloud thing had never happened before! The valley always enjoyed good weather — rain to make the crops grow, a little snow so children could ride their sleds, wind so they could fly kites, and sunshine to make everyone happy. As long as anyone could remember, the weather had been a friend and NOW it had changed. NO ONE knew what to do!

People beat on the weatherman's door demanding that he explain what had happened. Even more people DEMANDED he make the cloud go away. Alas, the weatherman could neither explain the cloud nor make it go away.

The mayor declared a state of emergency. She called an urgent meeting in the Holiday Valley Town Hall. The oldest to the youngest attended, even the animals.

Everyone talked at once. The mayor banged her gavel at least 50 times to get their attention and the town crier screamed "ATTENTION!"

"You all must remember your manners."

Embarrassed, everyone grew quiet and the mayor spoke. She asked for suggestions from the Olders on the Holiday Council. They always had answers before, but this time they did not. Then the mayor asked the people what they thought. Many gave suggestions:

The policewoman thought she could arrest the cloud away ... but she could not.

The fireman thought he could water it away ... but he could not.

The doctor thought she could cure it away ... but she could not.

The dentist thought he could drill it away ... but he could not.

The politician thought he could promise it away ... but he could not.

The lawyer thought she could argue it away ... but she could not.

The banker thought she could interest it away ... but she could not.

The plumber thought he could drain it away ... but he could not.

The TV producer thought he could offer the cloud a starring role in a TV show, but all the people answered, "NO."

The cook thought he could cook it away … but he could not.

The teacher thought he could "teach it away" but he could not.

The mathematician, engineer and scientist thought they could explain it away … but they could not.

Finally when they had exhausted all their ideas, the people grew discouraged for this was the first time in Holiday Valley history that a problem could not be solved.

Merry said, "Olders, Sir and Ma'am, may we please speak?"

Oh my, every Older turned with wide eyes. This was unheard of! Children did not speak at official Holiday Valley meetings. However, after much consternation and discussion the Olders granted permission.

"Honorable Olders, the cloud probably comes from a faraway land. Maybe we could ask the cloud why it is here and what it wants."

"Yes, yes," everyone cried. "That is a splendid idea! Let's go and ask the cloud why it is here and what it wants from us."

They decided to choose a delegation to represent the valley, but NO ONE wanted to be left behind.

The whole valley decided to go to the mountain with Merry and Christmas leading the way. They found ropes and tied everyone together, so no one would be lost. The animals wanted to come, so the people tied ropes on them too.

After many hours they reached the top of the mountain and in one big voice they yelled, "Mr. Cloud," (they were polite) "please, please, tell us why you have traveled to our valley and what do you want from us?"

For a few minutes the cloud remained quiet and all held their breath.

Then the cloud spoke ... and everyone let out a breath in relief.

"People of Holiday Valley ... you are fortunate ... you are happy, you have no big problems, you help one another and most of the time you do what is right."

Everyone was pleased to hear this.

The mayor said, "Why thank you, Mr. Cloud ... you are more than welcome here. You can stay and live with us. Just don't be so dense, cold, and smelly."

Mayor
Happy
Valley

"NO," the cloud rumbled. "That is NOT what I want from you! It would be nice to stay awhile, but that is not why I came. I have been sent for a very special purpose. In this valley there is much happiness and joy and sharing with one another ... and that is good."

The people of Holiday Valley, happy to hear this, smiled. Then the cloud said, "BUT you have done ONE THING wrong, one BAD thing."

"Oh my," they all gasped. "What could it be?" They did not understand. How could they have done something so BAD and not know it?

"Please Mr. Cloud, what have we done wrong? We are sorry for anything that is wrong. Please tell us what it is."

Mr. Cloud replied, "You have not found a way to share your happiness and teach the OUTSIDE what you know about being friends and taking care of one another! You have become selfish. YOU MUST FIND A WAY TO SHARE, to bring joy and happiness to the OUTSIDE ... especially to the children who so need it. I will not go away until you have found something to share with all."

They held a meeting at the bottom of the mountain.

The baker said, "I could bake wonderful cookies and send them OUTSIDE."

The candy maker said, "I could make candy canes."

The dressmaker said, "I could make stockings."

The toymaker said, "I could make toys."

The glassmaker said, "I could make bright shiny bulbs."

The cloud listened, "This sounds good but ... we still need something else ..."

The cook said, "I could make special dinners."

The lumberjack said, "I could send special evergreen trees to the OUTSIDE."

The musician and songwriter said, "We could write special music and send it."

The cloud listened to the many suggestions. Finally, Merry and Christmas asked to speak. "Sir Cloud, Miss Mayor, Council Olders, may we speak?"

"Yes," the mayor answered.

"Why don't we declare a special Happy Holiday Valley Day and take all the gifts and deliver them to all the children and give them cards with happy holiday wishes?"

Then the chief reindeer spoke up, "We reindeer, with our elf friends, can help deliver them to the children of the world."

Uncle Jolly who knew the most about the OUTSIDE immediately said he would show the way and drive the magic sleigh so they could deliver in one night.

Everyone jumped up and down and shouted to be heard. Such excitement for all! It was joyous to see how many wanted to SHARE their talents and skills to make gifts for the world.

"We can make beautiful stockings of red and green — and gifts that go into them. We will work all year so that every child receives one," added the seamstresses, artists, and toymakers of Holiday Valley.

"And...don't forget we can make wonderful red and green cookies, candies, and chocolates to put in the stockings so every child has wonderful treats," the bakers, candy makers, and chocolatiers added.

"What about sending a tree ... a decorated tree that would have wonderful ornaments and pine cones and ribbons and all bright things with lights to show some of the delights of Holiday Valley," suggested the lumberjacks and ornament makers. "That would cheer people up!"

Finally the cloud roared its approval, "NOW THAT is what I am talking about. What a great way to share your love and joy with children who need it. That's the Holiday spirit I want to see."

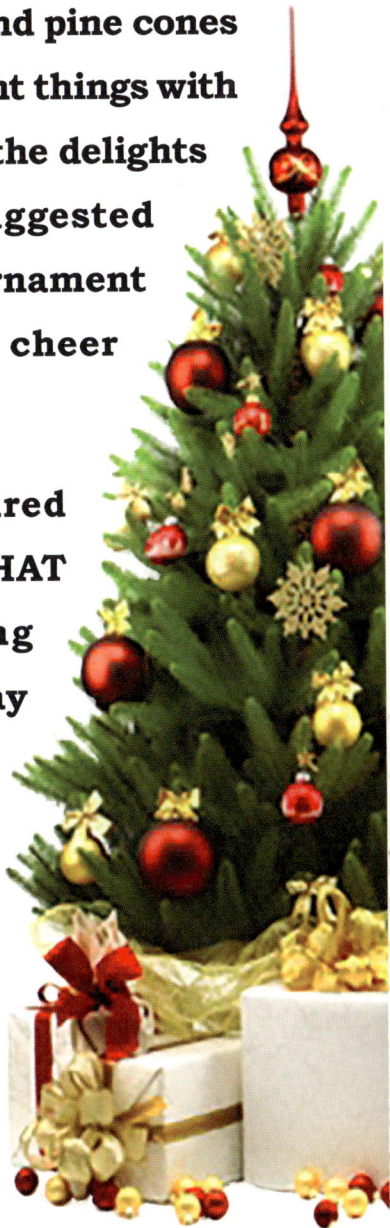

So right then and there, by unanimous decision and Mr. Cloud's approval, the mayor proclaimed a special mission from Holiday Valley to the OUTSIDE.

Since then, every December 25th, the gifts made by all of the children, adults, and animals of Holiday Valley are wrapped and delivered.

To honor the children, Merry and Christmas, the townspeople decided delivery day would be called:

Merry Christmas!

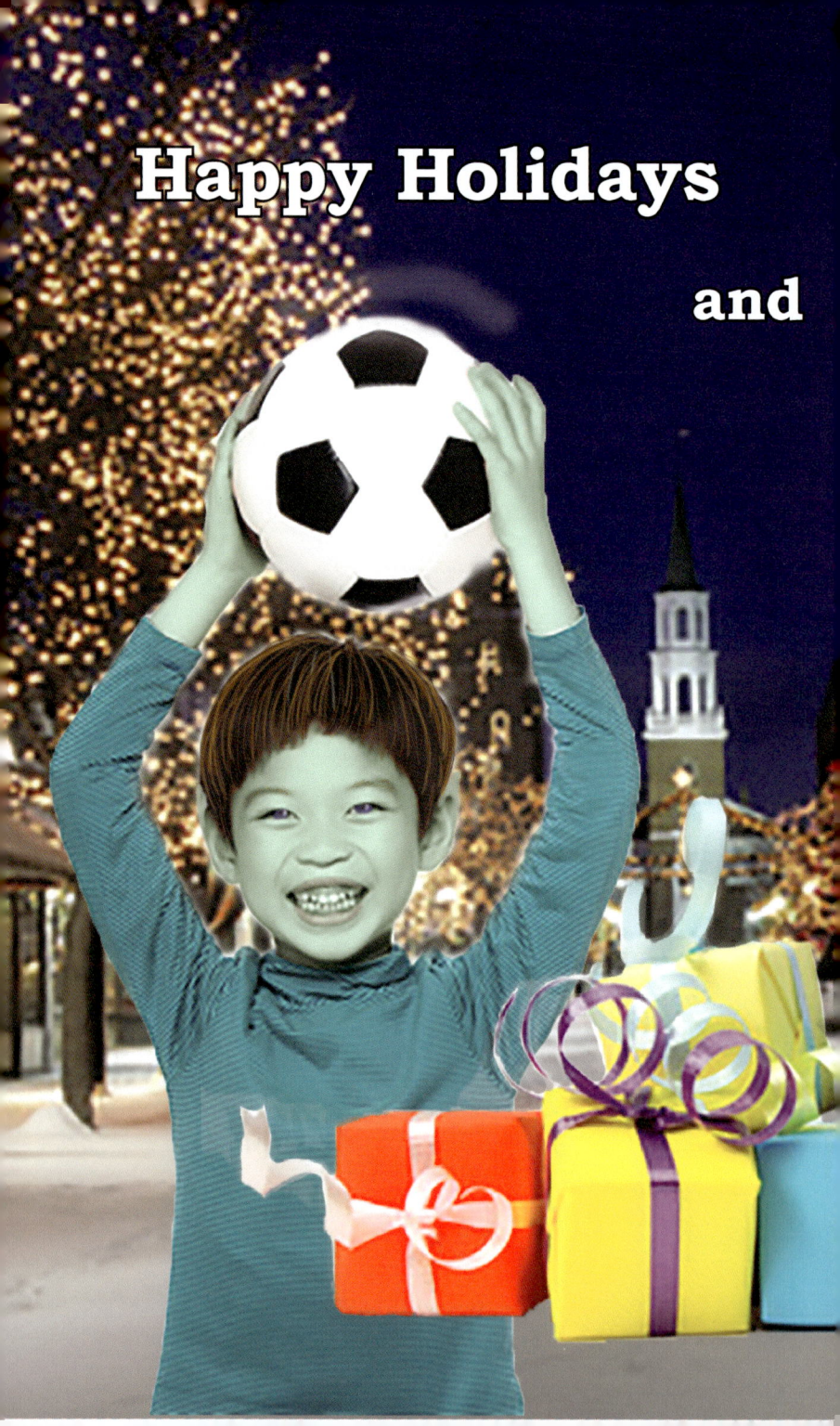

Happy Holidays

and

Merry Christmas

Dedication....

This book is dedicated to ALL in the world who have the Spirit of Holiday Valley residing in them. May the Gift of love, caring, and sharing be part of your life every day.

JoAnn R. Forrester

CPSIA information can be obtained
at www.ICGtesting.com
Printed in the USA
BVIC00n0942211114
374728BV00006B/1